Proof of Paternity

Proof of Paternity

*Are You a
Child of God?*

Pearl Nsiah-Kumi

ReadersMagnet, LLC

Proof of Paternity: Are You a Child of God?
Copyright © 2022 by Pearl Nsiah-Kumi

Published in the United States of America
ISBN Paperback: 978-1-957312-06-4
ISBN eBook: 978-1-956780-99-4

All rights reserved. No part of this publication may be reproduced, stored in a retrieval system or transmitted in any way by any means, electronic, mechanical, photocopy, recording or otherwise without the prior permission of the author except as provided by USA copyright law.

The opinions expressed by the author are not necessarily those of ReadersMagnet, LLC.

ReadersMagnet, LLC
10620 Treena Street, Suite 230 | San Diego, California, 92131 USA
1.619.354.2643 | www.readersmagnet.com

Book design copyright © 2022 by ReadersMagnet, LLC. All rights reserved.
Cover design by Ericka Obando
Interior design by Mary Mae Romero

Contents

Dedication vii

Acknowledgement ix

Introduction xi

Becoming a Child of God. 1

Proof of Sonship 3

Father-Child Relationship 5

Unfailing Love 6

    His Name is Like a Signed Blank Check to Meet Our Needs 6

    His Promise to Respond to Our Needs 6

    His Guarantees 7

Faithfulness Toward God 8

Living Godly Lives. 9

Loving the Brethren (Siblings) 9

Imitating the Siblings (Mature Siblings) 10

Sharing Our Faith............................ 12

Living Among Unbelievers.................... 13

Living in Expectation........................ 14

Conclusion 17

Contact Pearl Nsiah-Kumi 19

Other Books by Pearl Nsiah-Kumi 21

Dedication

This book—*Proof of Paternity*—is dedicated to my "Peeps": **Jane, Sharon, Thuy, Keiko, Kim, Bethanne, Carmen, Carole,** and **Ruby.** Thank you **ALL** for your love, support, and prayers.

Peeps, it is my prayer that we'll each continue to bear Godly fruit—the "proof" that we are, indeed, God's children… without question.

I love you!

Acknowledgement

Many thanks to my brother, **Dr. George Harton**, former President of the Washington Bible College and Capital Bible Seminary, for his ongoing support and love, and help in my writing efforts.

Dr. Harton, thank you! I love you!

Introduction

Quite often, it becomes necessary to find out who fathered a child. For obvious reasons, one doesn't have that concern about the mother—she delivered the baby. Proof is a necessity in a situation where the mother is unsure who fathered the baby because of having been in multiple relationships at the same time.

On other occasions, the mother states who she believes the father is, but that individual questions the legitimacy of the paternity. In either case, the only sure way to resolve these kinds of issues is to request DNA testing.

According to the Cleveland Clinic, *"paternity testing can determine whether or not a particular man is the biological father of a particular child."* The procedure involves collecting and examining the DNA of a small sample of bodily fluid or tissue from a child and the potential father. The result of the test proves once and for all the biological relationship between the child and the man.

Similarly, there is a way to determine who has God for a Father, but it is not through DNA testing. God has His own criteria. One has to meet those criteria in order to qualify as a child of God.

Are you a child of God?
What's your **proof?**

The Bible expresses a father/child relationship in several ways, and they all mean the same thing: One has to be born again or be adopted into the family of God. Once either happens, you become a child of God!

Becoming a Child of God

In order to become a child of God, you have to admit that you are a sinner, repent, and ask God (pray) for forgiveness through Jesus' shed blood.

Below are some of the ways the Bible describes that process:

- ❖ *"I tell you the truth; unless you are born again, you cannot see the Kingdom of God"* (John 3:3). (You have a change of heart toward God and sin.)
- ❖ *"This is how God loved the world: He gave His one and only Son so that everyone who believes in Him [Jesus] will not perish but have eternal life"* (John 3:16).
- ❖ *"God presented Jesus as the sacrifice for sin. People are made right with God when they believe that Jesus sacrificed His life, shedding His blood"* (Romans 3:25).
- ❖ *"If you openly declare that Jesus is Lord and believe in your heart that God raised Him from the dead, you will be saved"* (Romans 10:9).
- ❖ *"Christ has already accomplished the purpose for which the law was given. As a result, all who believe in Him are made right with God"* (Romans 10:4).

- ❖ *"Everyone who believes that Jesus is the Christ has become a child of God"* (1 John 5:1).
- ❖ *"Whoever has the Son has life; whoever does not have God's Son does not have life"* (1 John 5:12).

Proof of Sonship

When one believes in Jesus for salvation, he or she is indwelt by the Holy Spirit as assurance and proof of Sonship. Having respect for the Word of God, which leads to obedience is also confirmation that He is our Father.

Below are Scriptures that evidence Sonship:

- ❖ *"I will ask the Father, and He will give you another Advocate, who will not leave you. He is the Holy Spirit, who leads into all truth. But you know Him because He lives with you now and later will live in you"* (John 14:16-17).
- ❖ *"Anyone who does not have the Spirit of Christ does not belong to Him"* (Romans 8:9). (In other words, the believer has the Spirit of God.)
- ❖ *"God has testified about His Son. All who believe in the Son of God know in their hearts that this testimony is true"* (1 John 5:9-10).
- ❖ *"Those who obey God's commandments remain in fellowship with Him and He with them. And we know He lives in us because the Spirit He gave us lives in us"* (1 John 3:24).
- ❖ *"We call Him Abba, Father. For His Spirit joins with our spirit to affirm that we are God's children"* (Romans 8:15-16).

- ❖ Loving God's other children is also proof of paternity. *"Everyone who believes Jesus is the Christ has become a child of God. And everyone who loves the Father loves His children, too. We know we love God's children if we love God and obey His commandments"* (1 John 5:1-2).
- ❖ *"We can be sure that we know Him if we obey His commandments. If someone claims, 'I know God,' but doesn't obey God's commandments, that person is a liar and is not living in the truth. But those who obey God's Word truly show how completely they love Him. That is how we know we are living in Him"* (1 John 2:3-5).
- ❖ *"If you love Me, obey My commandments"* (John 14:15).
- ❖ *"Loving God means keeping His commandments; His commandments are not burdensome"* (1 John 5:3).
- ❖ *"You must live as God's obedient children. Don't slip back into your old ways of living to satisfy your own desire. You didn't know any better then. But now you must be holy in everything you do, just as God who chose you is Holy"* (1 Peter 1:15).

Father-Child Relationship

Quite often, once paternity is established, biological fathers find relationships with their child change for the better. Bonding improves, and it becomes a father/child relationship. Once paternity is established, many fathers take on the responsibility to meet the child's needs—physically, emotionally, and socially. Those needs would include food, shelter, clothing, education, and medical care. There is also the responsibility to correct and even reprimand the child as needed.

Likewise, the child has the responsibility to love, respect, and obey the father (depending on age) in any way possible. The child also has the duty and privilege of loving and caring for other members of the family.

Unfailing Love

Similarly, just as the human father provides for his child, when we become a child of God, He promises to provide and care for us. God the Father states:

"I will never fail you. I will never abandon you" (Hebrews 13:5).

****

His Name is Like a Signed Blank Check to Meet Our Needs

"You can ask for anything in My name, and I will do it so that the Son can bring glory to the Father. Yes, ask Me for anything in My name, and I will do it" (John 14:13-14).

His Promise to Respond to Our Needs

"Come to Me, all of you who are weary and carry heavy burdens, and I will give you rest" (Matthew 11:28).

"I will answer them before they even call to Me. While they are still talking about their needs, I will go ahead and answer their prayers" (Isaiah 65:24).

****

His Guarantees

God is faithful, and His nature doesn't change. We can trust His promises; they are as good as done!

"There is more than enough room in my Father's home. If this were not so, would I have told you that I am going to prepare a place for you? When everything is ready, I will come and get you, so that you will always be with Me where I am going" (John 14:2-3).

This is the guarantee for our eternal life in Heaven with God. Let's look forward to Him with expectancy.

Faithfulness Toward God

As Christians (children of God), He must be our first love and should have the first place in our lives, thoughts, and actions. We should not allow anything or anyone else on the throne of our hearts. We must examine ourselves continually, making sure we are giving Him His rightful place. He says in His Word:

"Dear children, keep away from anything that might take God's place in your hearts" (1 John 5:21).

"Imitate God, therefore, in everything you do, because you are His dear children. Live a life filled with love, following the example of Christ. He loved us and offered Himself as a sacrifice for us, a pleasing aroma to God" (Ephesians 5:1).

Living Godly Lives

God wants us to be holy like He is, to walk like He did! Our lives should imitate Him.

"God's children do not make a practice of sinning, for God's Son holds them securely, and the evil one cannot touch them. We know that we are children of God and that the world around us is under the control of the evil one" (1 John 5:18-19).

All children are disobedient now and then. What that verse is instructing us to do is not to make sin a habit. Sin interrupts our relationship with our Father, and practicing sin really shows that we don't love Him as we claim.

"I am the LORD your God. You must consecrate yourselves and be holy, because I am Holy" (Leviticus 11:44).

"Train yourself to be godly. Physical training is good, but training for godliness is much better, promising benefits in this life and in the life to come" (1 Timothy 4:7-8).

****

Loving the Brethren (Siblings)

In human families, siblings don't always get along for numerous reasons. Many times, minimal effort is made to reconcile. It should not be that way among the children of God because He commands us to love each other! Period.

"Love one another… If anyone claims, 'I am living in the light,' but hates a fellow believer, that person is still living in darkness. Anyone who loves a fellow believer is living in the light and does not cause others to stumble" (1 John 2:7, 9-10).

"This is His commandment: We must believe in the name of His Son, Jesus Christ, and love one another, just as He commanded us. Those who obey God's commandments remain in fellowship with Him and He with them. And we know He lives in us because the Spirit He gave us lives in us" (1 John 3:23-24).

"Let's not merely say that we love each other; let us show the truth by our actions" (1 John 3:22).

"Since God chose you to be the holy people He loves, you must clothe yourselves with tenderhearted mercy, kindness, humility, gentleness, and patience. Make allowance for each other's faults, and forgive anyone who offends you. Remember: The Lord forgave you, so you must forgive others. For as members of one body, you are called to live in peace and always be thankful" (Colossians 3:12-15).

"Let us continue to love one another, for love comes from God. Anyone who loves is a child of God and knows God. But anyone who does not love does not know God, for God is love" (1 John 4:7-8).

****

Imitating the Siblings (Mature Siblings)

Usually, responsible, older siblings help with the care of the younger ones in the family. The same should be true in the spiritual family. The younger Christians should learn from the matured. The Scriptures address that in the following ways:

"I became your father in Christ Jesus when I preached the Good News to you. So, I urge you to imitate me" (1 Corinthians 4:15-16).

"Remember your leaders who taught you the Word of God. Think of all the good that has come from their lives, and follow the example of their faith" (Hebrews 13:7).

"We urge you to warn those who are lazy. Encourage those who are timid. Take tender care of those who are weak. Be patient with everyone. See that no one pays back evil for evil, but always try to do good to each other and to all people" (1 Thessalonians 5:14-15).

Sharing Our Faith

Sharing our faith is letting others know what God has done in our own lives and can do in theirs as well. Witnessing is the response to our Father's command to *"Go!"* Jesus asked His disciples on many occasions to share the Gospel with others, which is the continuation of what He came to do. He said of Himself, *"The Spirit of the Lord is upon me, for He has anointed me to bring Good News to the poor"* (Luke 5:18).

"Go and announce to them that the Kingdom of Heaven is near" (Matthew 10:7).

"You will stand trial before governors. But this will be your opportunity to tell the rulers and other unbelievers about Me" (Matthew 10:18).

"Go into all the world and preach the Good News to everyone. Anyone who believes and is baptized will be saved. But anyone who refused to believe will be condemned" (Mark 16:16).

We need to take these commands seriously as proof of our obedience to the Father. In addition, we need to show concern for unbelievers because if they stay in that condition much longer, the result would be disastrous: **Hell.**

Living Among Unbelievers

If you've become a Christian, know that this world is not the Christian's home; we are looking forward to living in Heaven with God and each other forever in the future. This world is a temporary place; therefore, we need to live as such and let those around us see how differently we live. Since we know the end of those who do not have a relationship with Jesus—Hell—our godly lives will be a witness to them. Our lives should make them want to know our Savior for whom we live so differently.

"Live wisely among those who are not believers, and make the most of every opportunity. Let your conversation be gracious and attractive, so that you will have the right response for everyone" (Colossians 4:5-6).

"You are the salt of the Earth. But what good is salt if it has lost its flavor? You are the light of the world—like a city on a hill, it cannot be hidden. In the same way, let your good deeds shine out for all to see so that everyone will praise your Heavenly Father" (Matthew 5:13-16).

"If your enemies are hungry, feed them. If they are thirsty, give them drink. Don't let evil conquer you, but conquer evil by doing good" (Romans 12:20-21).

Living in Expectation

When parents go to work, their children look forward to them returning home. I remember when my younger daughter would always stand at the daycare door, waiting for me to come and pick her up.

Jesus promised us that He will return to take us home to Heaven. Since He is faithful, we believe He's really coming back…and soon! We need to live in expectation of our Savior's return any day now!

While we live in expectation, we also need to be doing things right, especially since we don't know the day of Christ's return. We want to be doing things right when He appears so that we'll have nothing of which to be ashamed.

"When everything is ready, I will come and get you, so that you will always be with Me where I am" (John 14:2-3).

"You also must be ready all the time, for the Son of Man will come when least expected" (Luke 12:40).

"The day of the Lord's return will come unexpectedly like a thief in the night" (1 Thessalonians 5:2).

"In the future, you will see the Son of Man seated in the place of power at God's right hand, and coming on the clouds of Heaven" (Matthew 26:64).

Is God your Father? If not, there's only one other who could be your father: the devil! Examine your life. Whose nature do you have? If you live contrary to the Word of God, you no doubt have the nature of the devil.

As Jesus talked to the crowd and accused them of imitating their real father—the devil (see John 8:41)—they disagreed with Him. He then challenged them:

"If God were your Father, you would love Me because I have come to you from God. For you are the children of your father, the devil, and you love to do the evil things he does. He was a murderer from the beginning. He has always hated the truth because there is no truth in him. When he lies, it is consistent with his character, for he is a liar and the father of lies. Anyone who belongs to God listens gladly to the words of God. But you don't listen because you don't belong to God" (John 8:42-47).

Conclusion

You don't have to be or remain unsure of your relationship with God. You definitely don't have to be a child of the devil. You can put your faith in Jesus today or any day, as long as you are alive and Jesus has not returned to Earth.

You don't have as much control over your life as you may think. Anything can change at any time, so I urge you to call on Jesus today to ensure you've left the devil's camp of darkness and entered into God's light. You will then become a child of God, indwelt by the Holy Spirit. You will also know the difference in your heart and your life. For one, your priorities will change. Your love for God and the Church will grow, and you'll be more conscious of sin in your personal life and environment.

The Apostle Paul explains it this way:

"Anyone who belongs to Christ has become a new person. The old life is gone; a new life has begun" (2 Corinthians 5:17).

These changes will be proof that you're a child of God the Father.

On the other hand, if you are a Christian who is struggling with doubt or are unsure of your salvation, please reread this book and allow the Holy Spirit to help you settle the issue of Sonship and your responsibilities for good!

Contact Pearl Nsiah-Kumi

On the Web: www.pearlkumi.com
Via Email: pearl@pearlkumi.com

Other Books by Pearl Nsiah-Kumi

(Available for purchase at: www.pearlkumi.com/bookstore1

Get on Board and Stay on Board
The Last Train at Sunset
Time is Running Out
El Tiempo Se Esta Acabando
(Spanish version of Time is Running Out)
Living for Jesus Until He Returns
Prepare to Meet Your Maker
Your Maker is Your Husband
From the Garden to Eternity

Comments about your reading experience are welcome and appreciated. Please visit Pearl Nsiah-Kumi on her website or send her an email.

CPSIA information can be obtained
at www.ICGtesting.com
Printed in the USA
LVHW040317290322
714677LV00007B/522